IDW STAR TREK

JOHNSON
MOLNAR

EXPLORE STRANGE NEW WORLDS!

ENLIST IN STARFLEET

WRITER
MIKE JOHNSON

ARTIST
STEPHEN MOLNAR AND JOE PHILLIPS

COLORIST
JOHN RAUCH

LETTERER
NEIL UYETAKE

BASED ON THE ORIGINAL TELEPLAY OF *THE GALILEO SEVEN* BY
SAMUEL A. PEEPLES AND SHIMON WINCELBERG

CREATIVE CONSULTANT
ROBERTO ORCI

EDITOR
SCOTT DUNBIER

Visit us at www.abdopublishing.com

Reinforced library bound editions published in 2014 by Spotlight, a division of the ABDO Group, PO Box 398166, Minneapolis, MN 55439. Spotlight produces high-quality reinforced library bound editions for schools and libraries. Published by agreement with IDW.

Printed in the United States of America, North Mankato, Minnesota.
042013
092013
This book contains at least 10% recycled material.

STAR TREK created by Gene Roddenberry.
Special thanks to Risa Kessler and John Van Citters of CBS Consumer Products for their invaluable assistance.

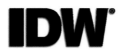

Library of Congress Cataloging-in-Publication Data

Johnson, Mike.
The Galileo Seven / story by Mike Johnson ; art by Stephen Molnar.
volumes cm. -- (Star Trek)
ISBN 978-1-61479-159-1 (part 1) -- ISBN 978-1-61479-160-7 (part 2)
1. Graphic novels. I. Molnar, Stephen, illustrator. II. Title.
PZ7.7.J6417Gal 2014
741.5'973--dc23

2013004266

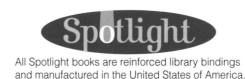

All Spotlight books are reinforced library bindings and manufactured in the United States of America.

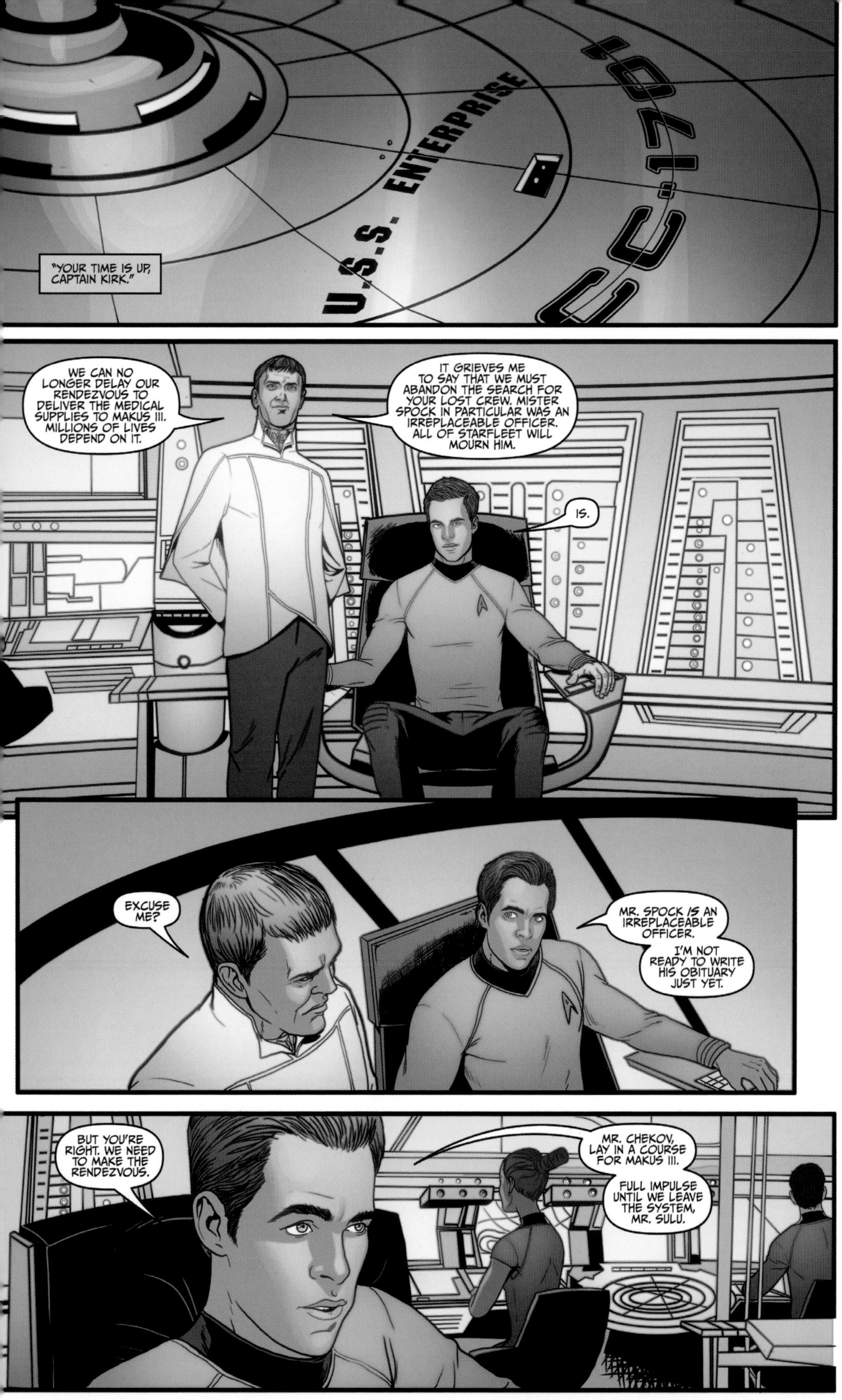

U.S.S. ENTERPRISE
NCC-1701
"YOUR TIME IS UP, CAPTAIN KIRK."
WE CAN NO LONGER DELAY OUR RENDEZVOUS TO DELIVER THE MEDICAL SUPPLIES TO MAKUS III. MILLIONS OF LIVES DEPEND ON IT.
IT GRIEVES ME TO SAY THAT WE MUST ABANDON THE SEARCH FOR YOUR LOST CREW. MISTER SPOCK IN PARTICULAR WAS AN IRREPLACEABLE OFFICER. ALL OF STARFLEET WILL MOURN HIM.
IS.
EXCUSE ME?
MR. SPOCK *IS* AN IRREPLACEABLE OFFICER.
I'M NOT READY TO WRITE HIS OBITUARY JUST YET.
BUT YOU'RE RIGHT. WE NEED TO MAKE THE RENDEZVOUS.
MR. CHEKOV, LAY IN A COURSE FOR MAKUS III.
FULL IMPULSE UNTIL WE LEAVE THE SYSTEM, MR. SULU.

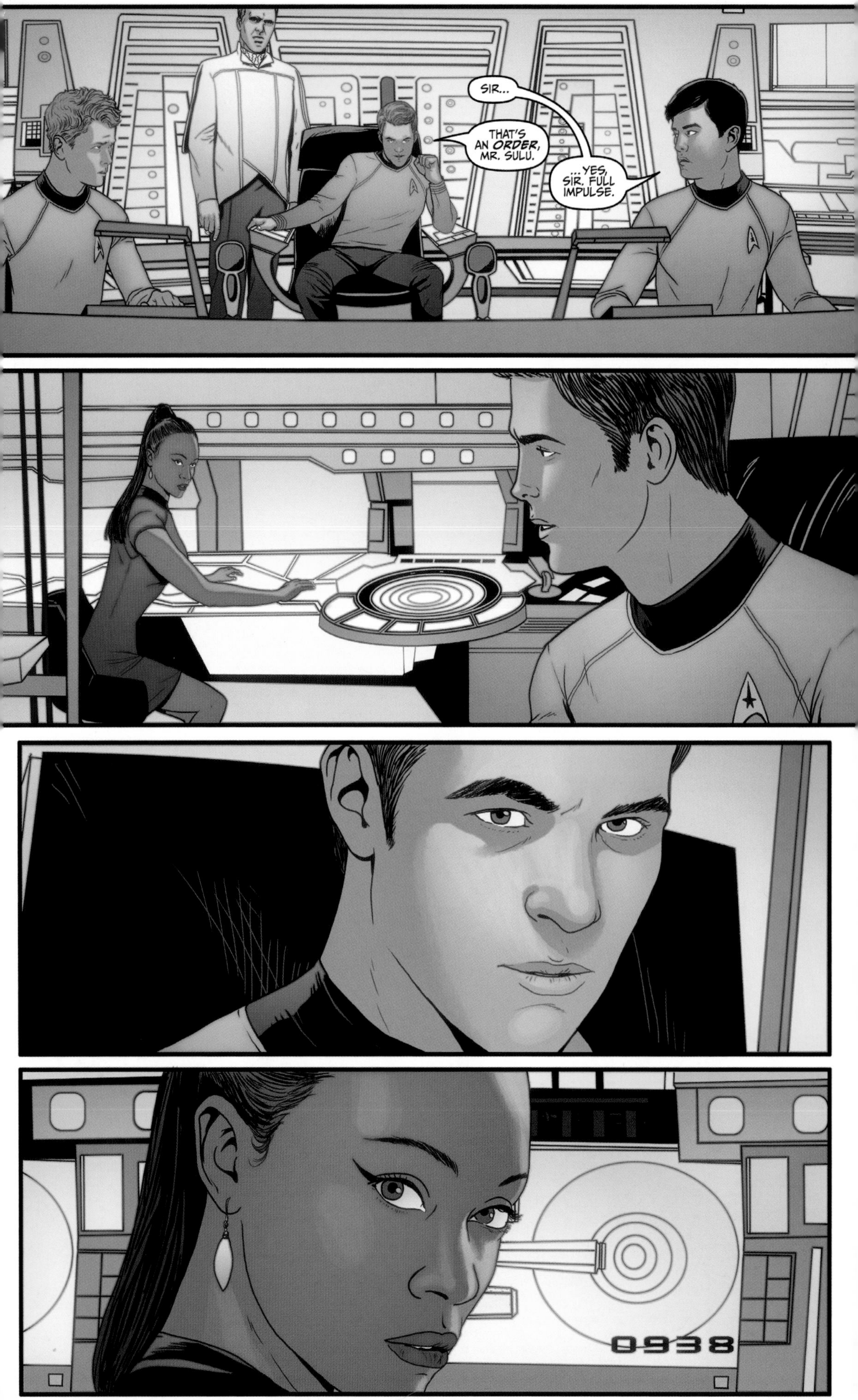
SIR...
THAT'S AN ORDER, MR. SULU.
...YES, SIR. FULL IMPULSE.
0938

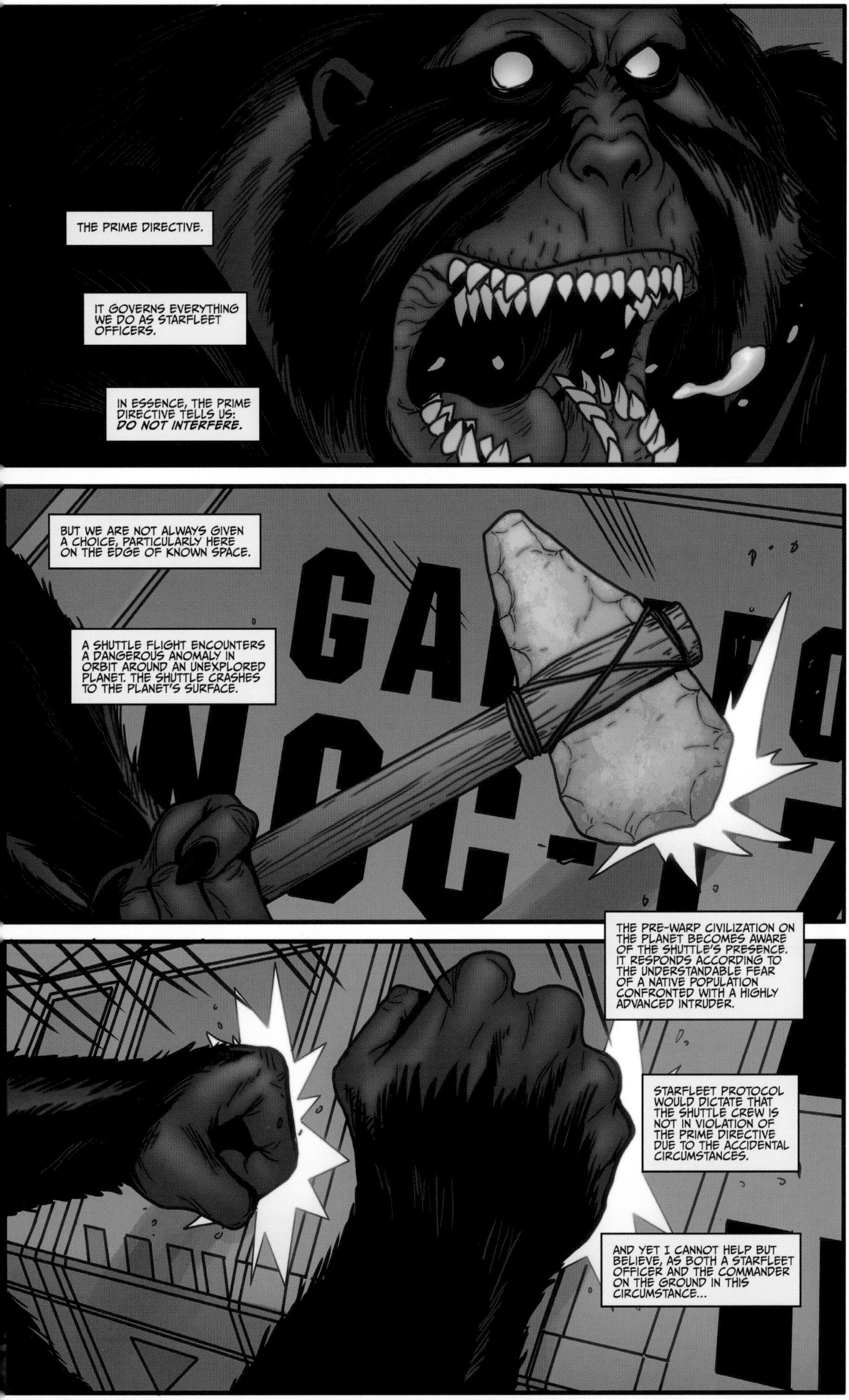
THE PRIME DIRECTIVE.
IT GOVERNS EVERYTHING WE DO AS STARFLEET OFFICERS.
IN ESSENCE, THE PRIME DIRECTIVE TELLS US: *DO NOT INTERFERE.*
BUT WE ARE NOT ALWAYS GIVEN A CHOICE, PARTICULARLY HERE ON THE EDGE OF KNOWN SPACE.
A SHUTTLE FLIGHT ENCOUNTERS A DANGEROUS ANOMALY IN ORBIT AROUND AN UNEXPLORED PLANET. THE SHUTTLE CRASHES TO THE PLANET'S SURFACE.
THE PRE-WARP CIVILIZATION ON THE PLANET BECOMES AWARE OF THE SHUTTLE'S PRESENCE. IT RESPONDS ACCORDING TO THE UNDERSTANDABLE FEAR OF A NATIVE POPULATION CONFRONTED WITH A HIGHLY ADVANCED INTRUDER.
STARFLEET PROTOCOL WOULD DICTATE THAT THE SHUTTLE CREW IS NOT IN VIOLATION OF THE PRIME DIRECTIVE DUE TO THE ACCIDENTAL CIRCUMSTANCES.
AND YET I CANNOT HELP BUT BELIEVE, AS BOTH A STARFLEET OFFICER AND THE COMMANDER ON THE GROUND IN THIS CIRCUMSTANCE...

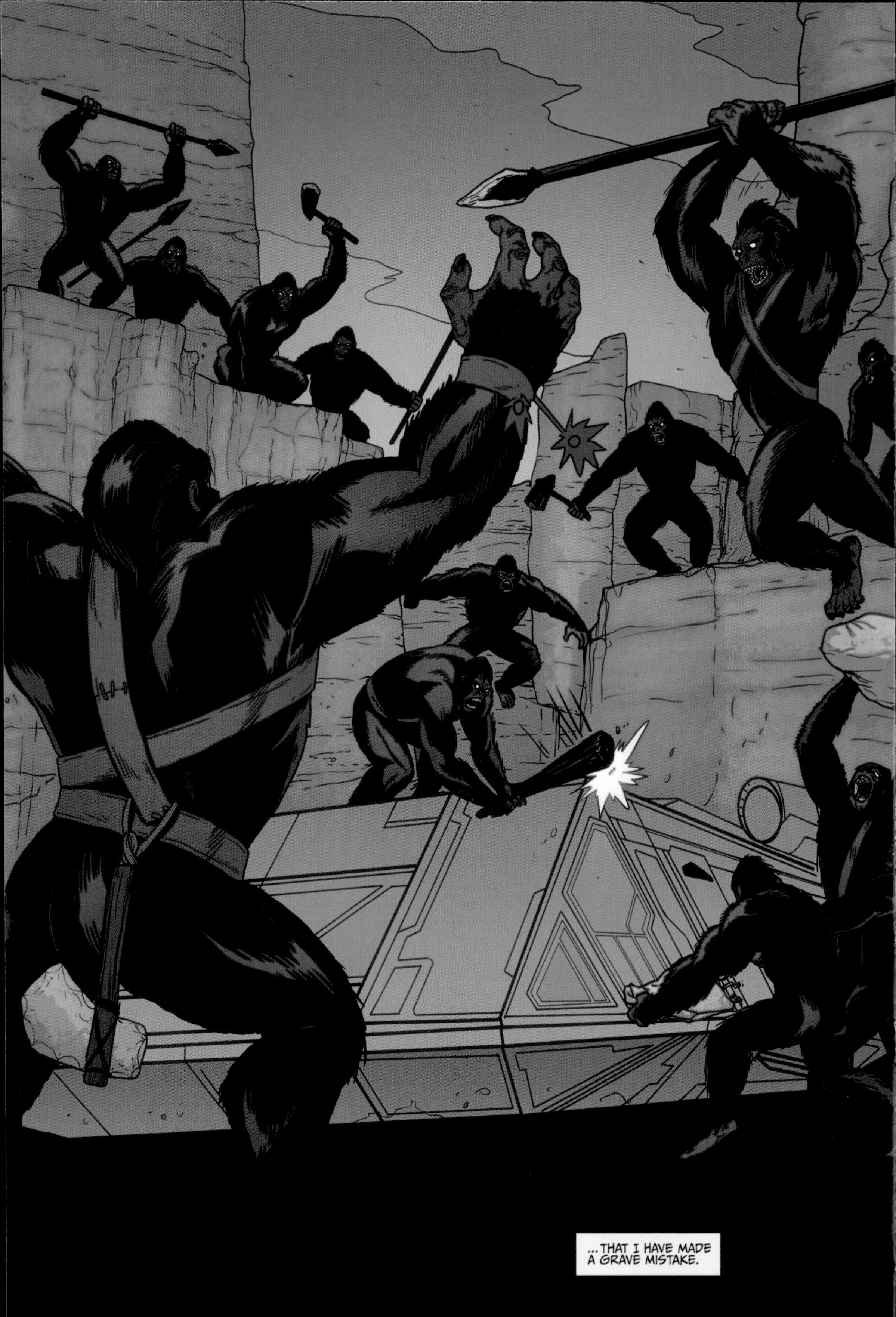
...THAT I HAVE MADE A GRAVE MISTAKE.

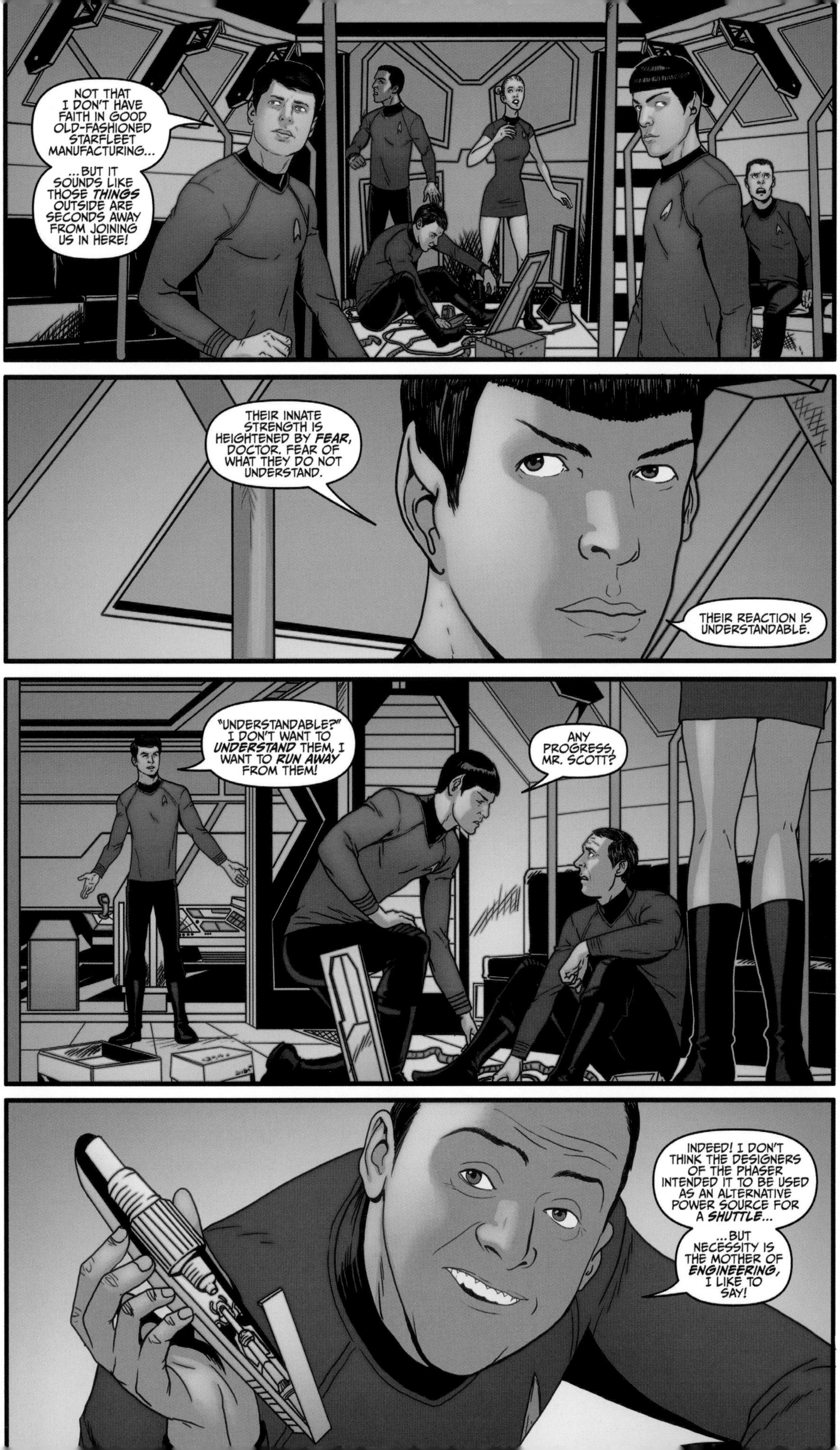
NOT THAT I DON'T HAVE FAITH IN GOOD OLD-FASHIONED STARFLEET MANUFACTURING...
...BUT IT SOUNDS LIKE THOSE *THINGS* OUTSIDE ARE SECONDS AWAY FROM JOINING US IN HERE!
THEIR INNATE STRENGTH IS HEIGHTENED BY *FEAR*, DOCTOR. FEAR OF WHAT THEY DO NOT UNDERSTAND.
THEIR REACTION IS UNDERSTANDABLE.
"UNDERSTANDABLE?" I DON'T WANT TO *UNDERSTAND* THEM, I WANT TO *RUN AWAY* FROM THEM!
ANY PROGRESS, MR. SCOTT?
INDEED! I DON'T THINK THE DESIGNERS OF THE PHASER INTENDED IT TO BE USED AS AN ALTERNATIVE POWER SOURCE FOR A *SHUTTLE*...
...BUT NECESSITY IS THE MOTHER OF *ENGINEERING*, I LIKE TO SAY!

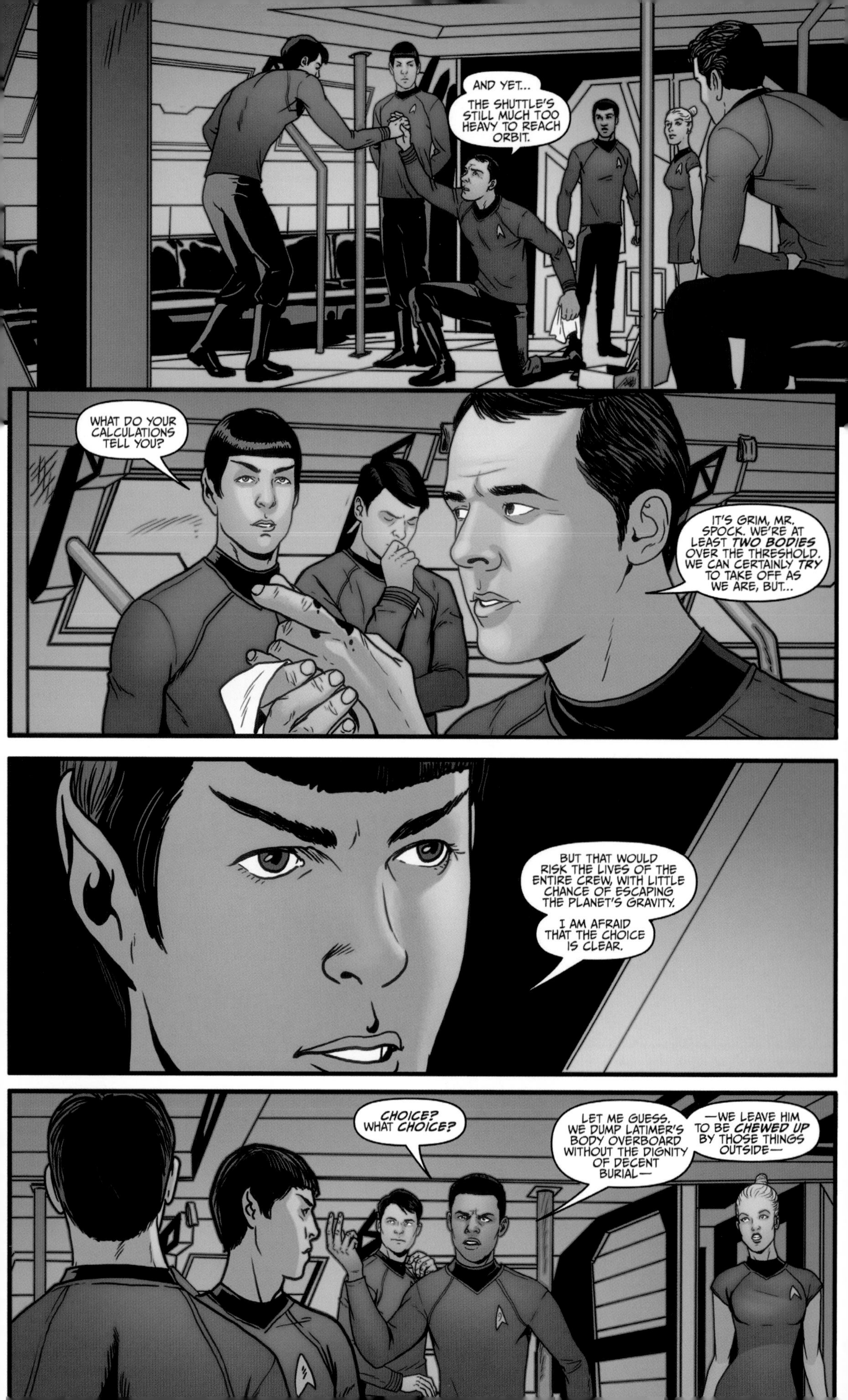
AND YET...
THE SHUTTLE'S STILL MUCH TOO HEAVY TO REACH ORBIT.
WHAT DO YOUR CALCULATIONS TELL YOU?
IT'S GRIM, MR. SPOCK. WE'RE AT LEAST *TWO BODIES* OVER THE THRESHOLD. WE CAN CERTAINLY *TRY* TO TAKE OFF AS WE ARE, BUT...
BUT THAT WOULD RISK THE LIVES OF THE ENTIRE CREW, WITH LITTLE CHANCE OF ESCAPING THE PLANET'S GRAVITY.
I AM AFRAID THAT THE CHOICE IS CLEAR.
CHOICE? WHAT *CHOICE?*
LET ME GUESS. WE DUMP LATIMER'S BODY OVERBOARD WITHOUT THE DIGNITY OF DECENT BURIAL—
—WE LEAVE HIM TO BE *CHEWED UP* BY THOSE THINGS OUTSIDE—

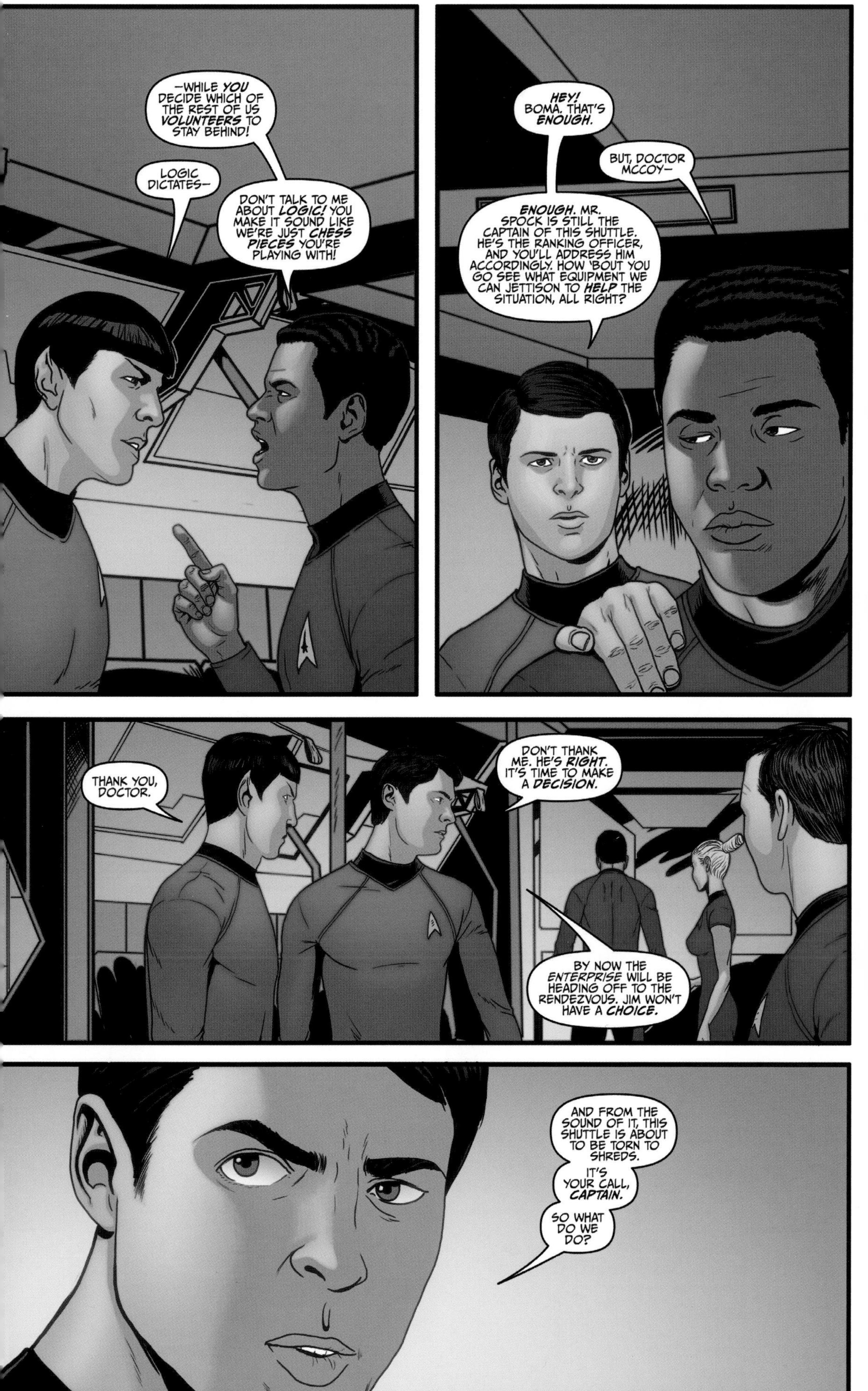
—WHILE YOU DECIDE WHICH OF THE REST OF US VOLUNTEERS TO STAY BEHIND!
LOGIC DICTATES—
DON'T TALK TO ME ABOUT LOGIC! YOU MAKE IT SOUND LIKE WE'RE JUST CHESS PIECES YOU'RE PLAYING WITH!
HEY! BOMA. THAT'S ENOUGH.
BUT, DOCTOR MCCOY—
ENOUGH. MR. SPOCK IS STILL THE CAPTAIN OF THIS SHUTTLE. HE'S THE RANKING OFFICER, AND YOU'LL ADDRESS HIM ACCORDINGLY. HOW 'BOUT YOU GO SEE WHAT EQUIPMENT WE CAN JETTISON TO HELP THE SITUATION, ALL RIGHT?
THANK YOU, DOCTOR.
DON'T THANK ME. HE'S RIGHT. IT'S TIME TO MAKE A DECISION.
BY NOW THE ENTERPRISE WILL BE HEADING OFF TO THE RENDEZVOUS. JIM WON'T HAVE A CHOICE.
AND FROM THE SOUND OF IT, THIS SHUTTLE IS ABOUT TO BE TORN TO SHREDS.
IT'S YOUR CALL, CAPTAIN.
SO WHAT DO WE DO?

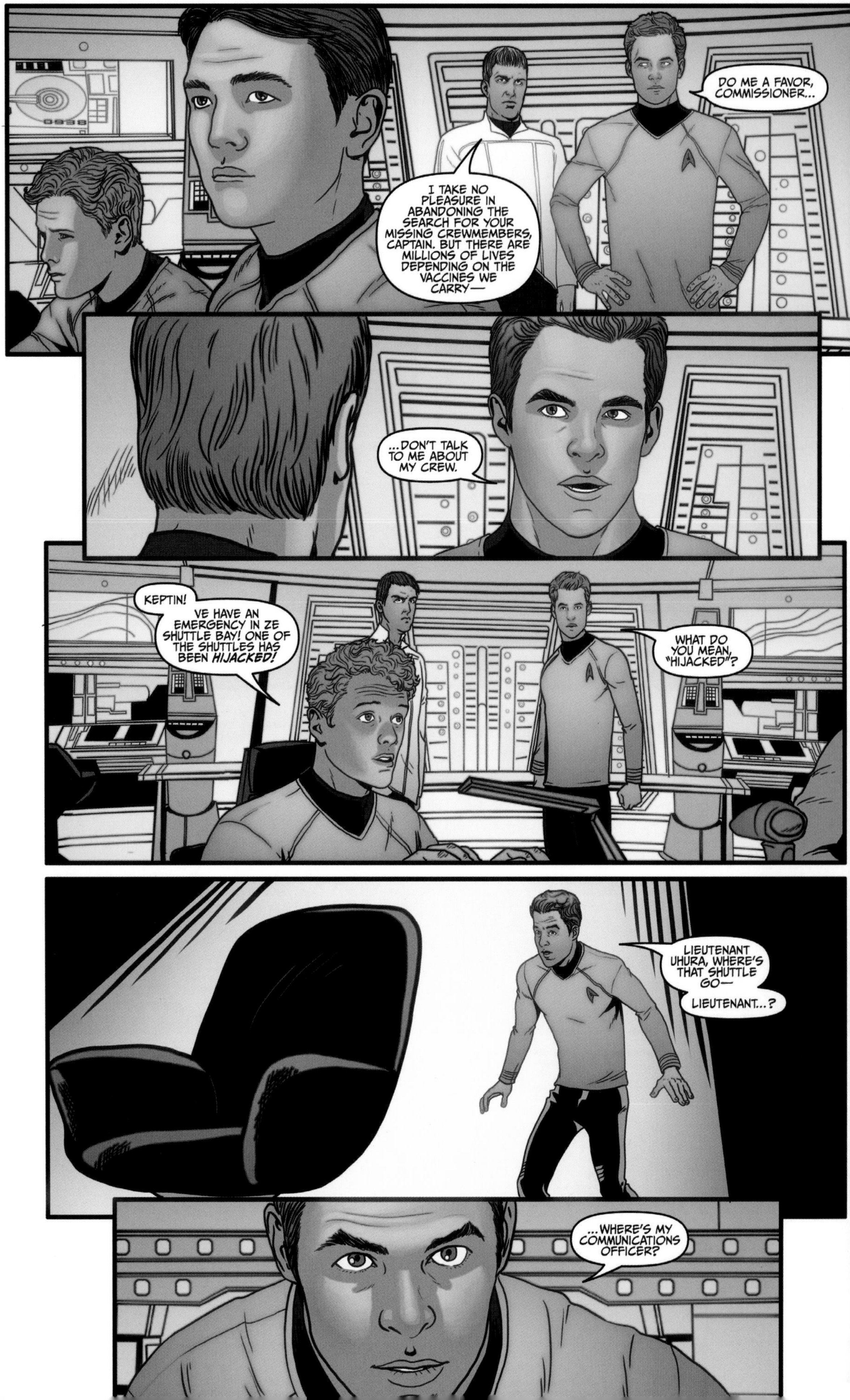
DO ME A FAVOR, COMMISSIONER...
I TAKE NO PLEASURE IN ABANDONING THE SEARCH FOR YOUR MISSING CREWMEMBERS, CAPTAIN. BUT THERE ARE MILLIONS OF LIVES DEPENDING ON THE VACCINES WE CARRY—
...DON'T TALK TO ME ABOUT MY CREW.
KEPTIN! VE HAVE AN EMERGENCY IN ZE SHUTTLE BAY! ONE OF THE SHUTTLES HAS BEEN HIJACKED!
WHAT DO YOU MEAN, "HIJACKED"?
LIEUTENANT UHURA, WHERE'S THAT SHUTTLE GO—
LIEUTENANT...?
...WHERE'S MY COMMUNICATIONS OFFICER?

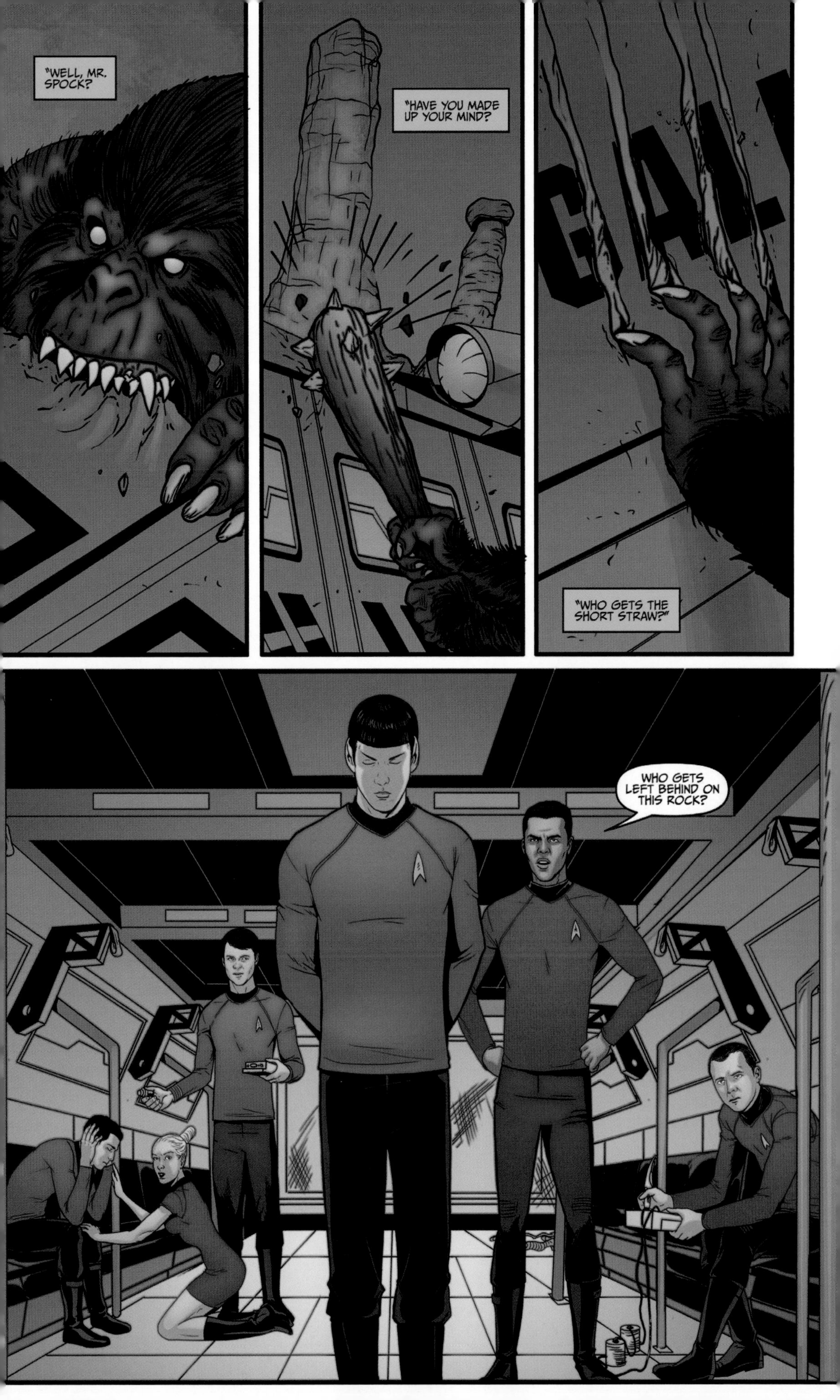
"WELL, MR. SPOCK?
"HAVE YOU MADE UP YOUR MIND?
"WHO GETS THE SHORT STRAW?"
WHO GETS LEFT BEHIND ON THIS ROCK?

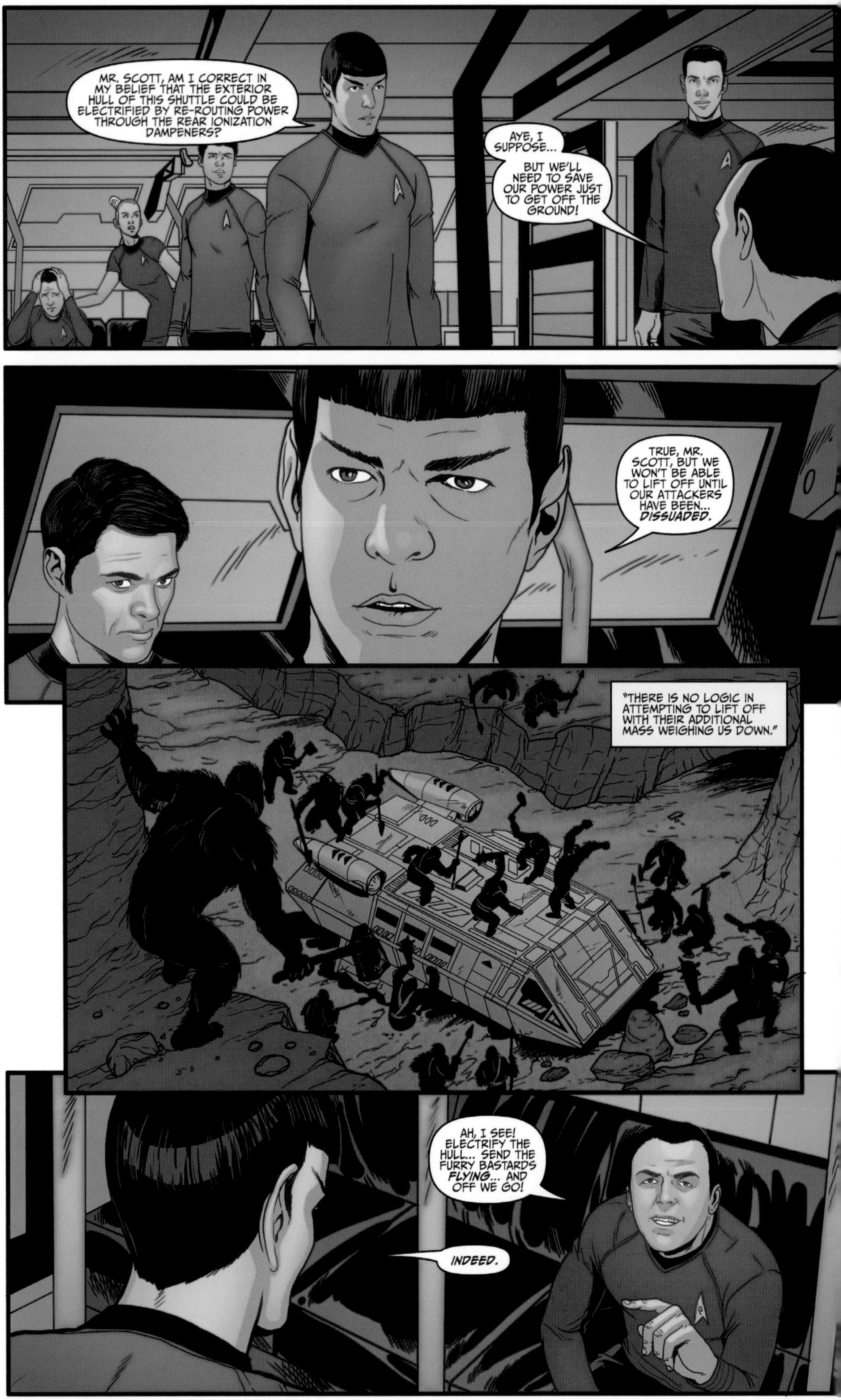
MR. SCOTT, AM I CORRECT IN MY BELIEF THAT THE EXTERIOR HULL OF THIS SHUTTLE COULD BE ELECTRIFIED BY RE-ROUTING POWER THROUGH THE REAR IONIZATION DAMPENERS?
AYE, I SUPPOSE...
BUT WE'LL NEED TO SAVE OUR POWER JUST TO GET OFF THE GROUND!
TRUE, MR. SCOTT, BUT WE WON'T BE ABLE TO LIFT OFF UNTIL OUR ATTACKERS HAVE BEEN... *DISSUADED*.
"THERE IS NO LOGIC IN ATTEMPTING TO LIFT OFF WITH THEIR ADDITIONAL MASS WEIGHING US DOWN."
AH, I SEE! ELECTRIFY THE HULL... SEND THE FURRY BASTARDS *FLYING*... AND OFF WE GO!
INDEED.

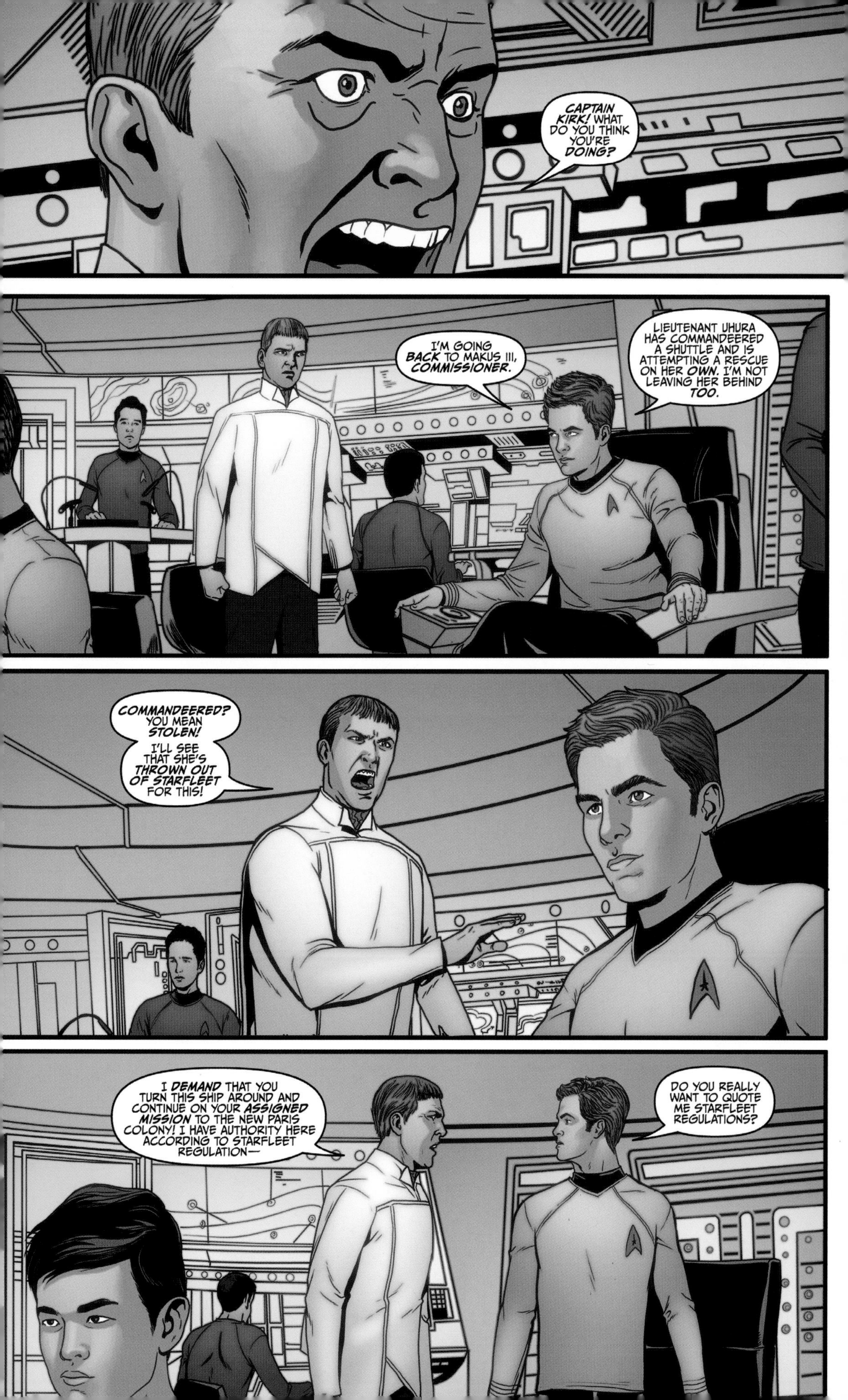
CAPTAIN KIRK! WHAT DO YOU THINK YOU'RE DOING?
I'M GOING BACK TO MAKUS III, COMMISSIONER.
LIEUTENANT UHURA HAS COMMANDEERED A SHUTTLE AND IS ATTEMPTING A RESCUE ON HER OWN. I'M NOT LEAVING HER BEHIND TOO.
COMMANDEERED? YOU MEAN STOLEN! I'LL SEE THAT SHE'S THROWN OUT OF STARFLEET FOR THIS!
I DEMAND THAT YOU TURN THIS SHIP AROUND AND CONTINUE ON YOUR ASSIGNED MISSION TO THE NEW PARIS COLONY! I HAVE AUTHORITY HERE ACCORDING TO STARFLEET REGULATION—
DO YOU REALLY WANT TO QUOTE ME STARFLEET REGULATIONS?

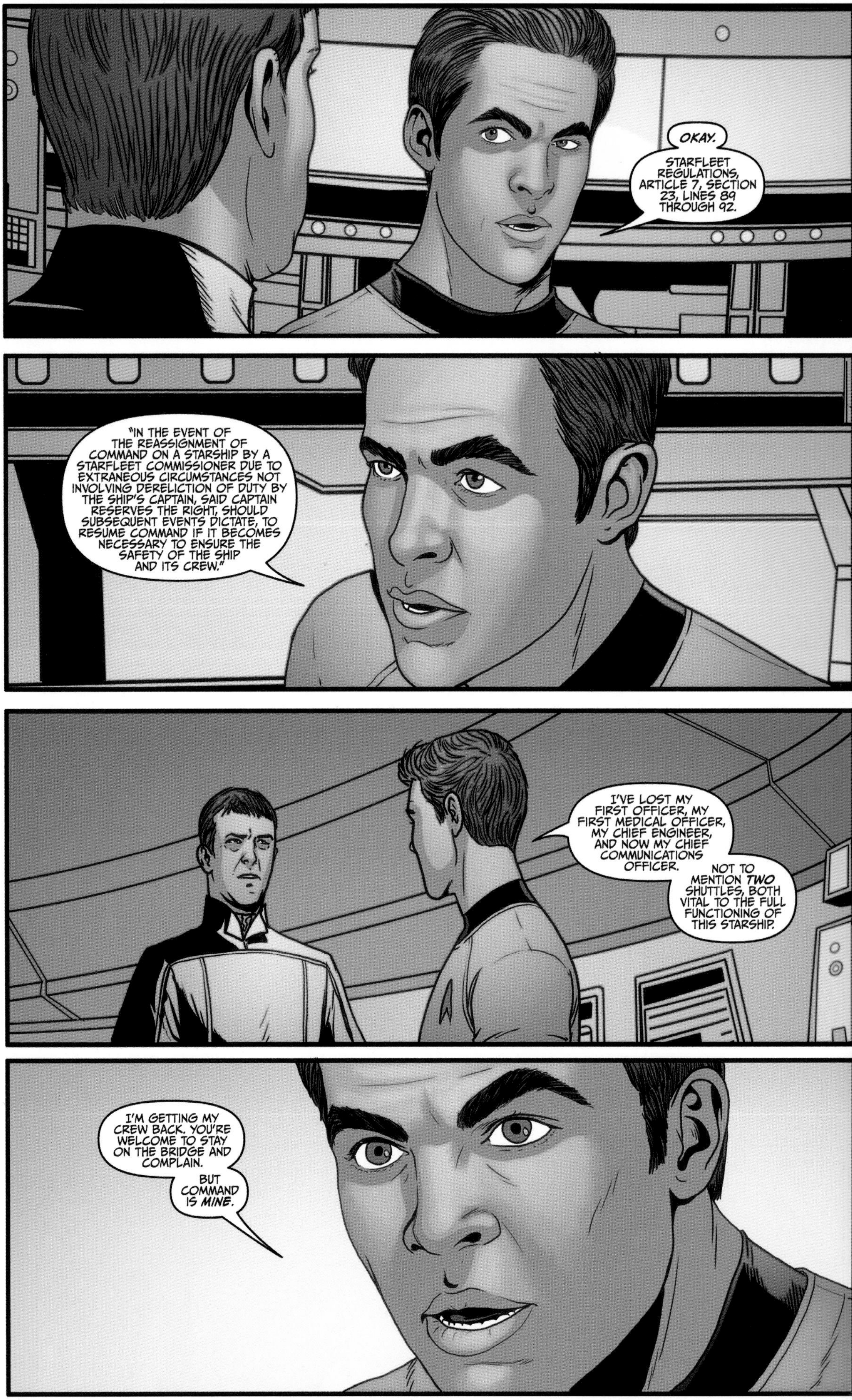
OKAY.
STARFLEET REGULATIONS, ARTICLE 7, SECTION 23, LINES 89 THROUGH 92.
"IN THE EVENT OF THE REASSIGNMENT OF COMMAND ON A STARSHIP BY A STARFLEET COMMISSIONER DUE TO EXTRANEOUS CIRCUMSTANCES NOT INVOLVING DERELICTION OF DUTY BY THE SHIP'S CAPTAIN, SAID CAPTAIN RESERVES THE RIGHT, SHOULD SUBSEQUENT EVENTS DICTATE, TO RESUME COMMAND IF IT BECOMES NECESSARY TO ENSURE THE SAFETY OF THE SHIP AND ITS CREW."
I'VE LOST MY FIRST OFFICER, MY FIRST MEDICAL OFFICER, MY CHIEF ENGINEER, AND NOW MY CHIEF COMMUNICATIONS OFFICER.
NOT TO MENTION *TWO* SHUTTLES, BOTH VITAL TO THE FULL FUNCTIONING OF THIS STARSHIP.
I'M GETTING MY CREW BACK. YOU'RE WELCOME TO STAY ON THE BRIDGE AND COMPLAIN.
BUT COMMAND IS *MINE*.

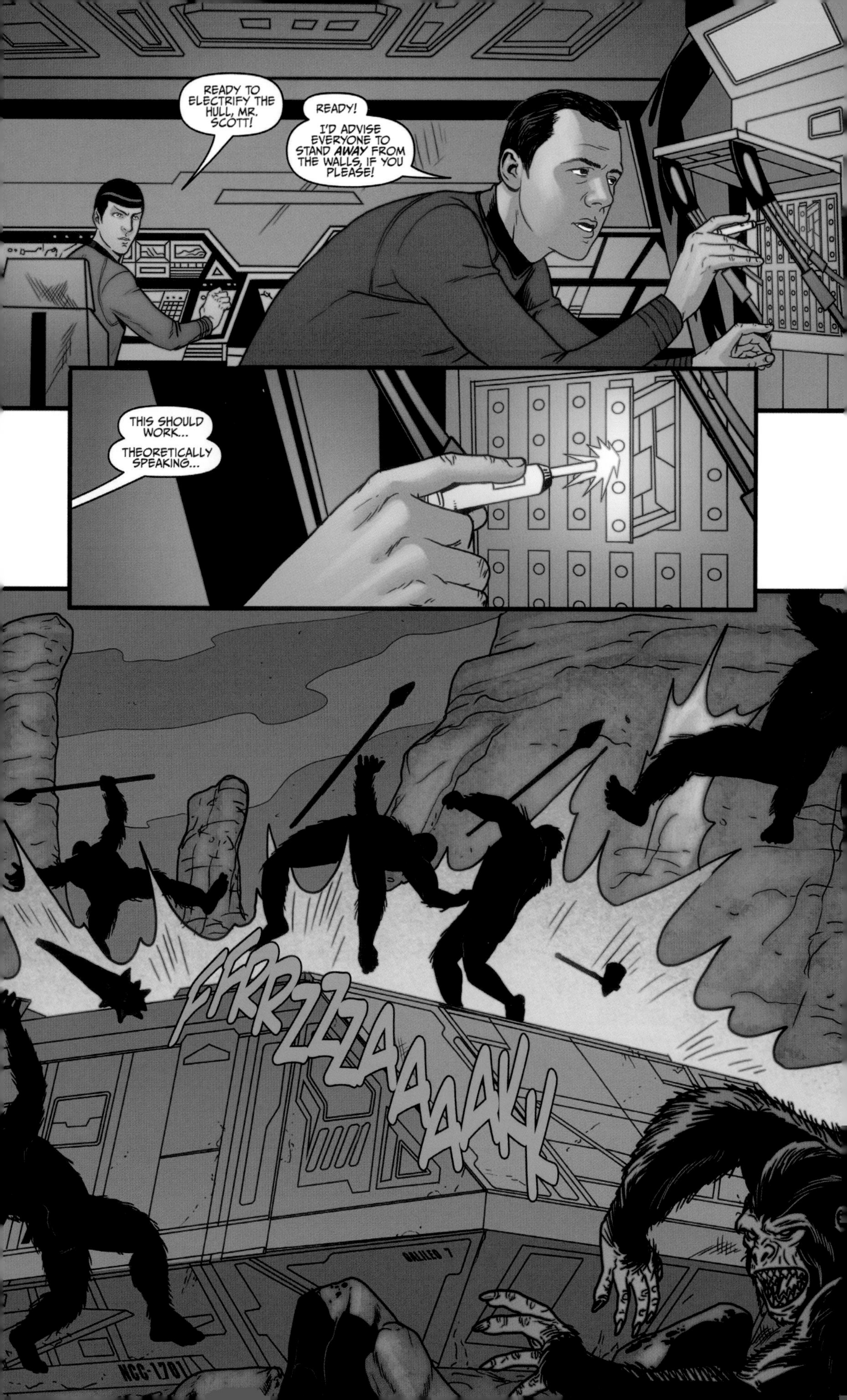
READY TO ELECTRIFY THE HULL, MR. SCOTT!
READY!
I'D ADVISE EVERYONE TO STAND AWAY FROM THE WALLS, IF YOU PLEASE!
THIS SHOULD WORK... THEORETICALLY SPEAKING...
ZFRRZZZAAAAKK
NCC-1701

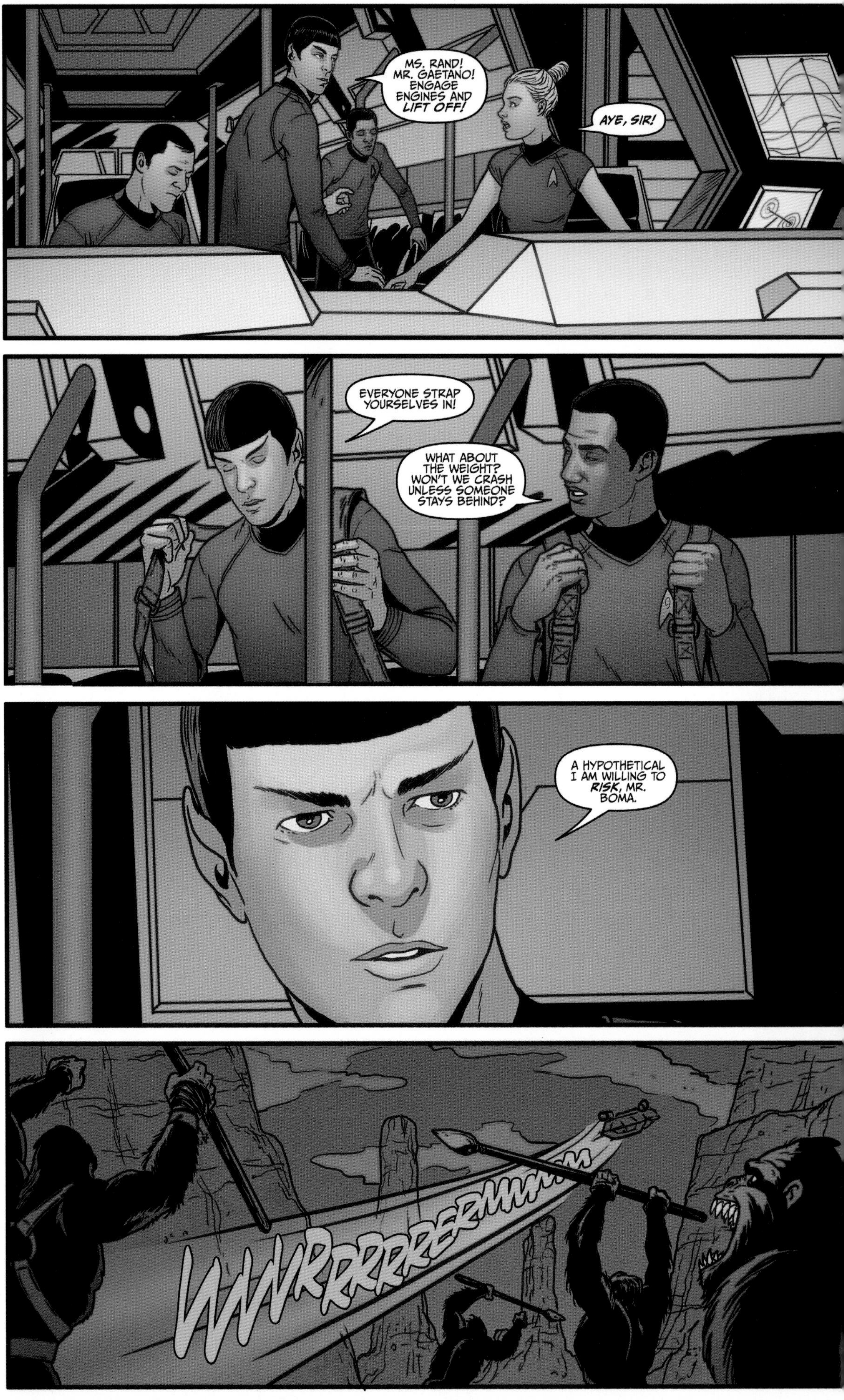
MS. RAND! MR. GAETANO! ENGAGE ENGINES AND LIFT OFF!
AYE, SIR!
EVERYONE STRAP YOURSELVES IN!
WHAT ABOUT THE WEIGHT? WON'T WE CRASH UNLESS SOMEONE STAYS BEHIND?
A HYPOTHETICAL I AM WILLING TO RISK, MR. BOMA.
WWRRRRRERMMMMM

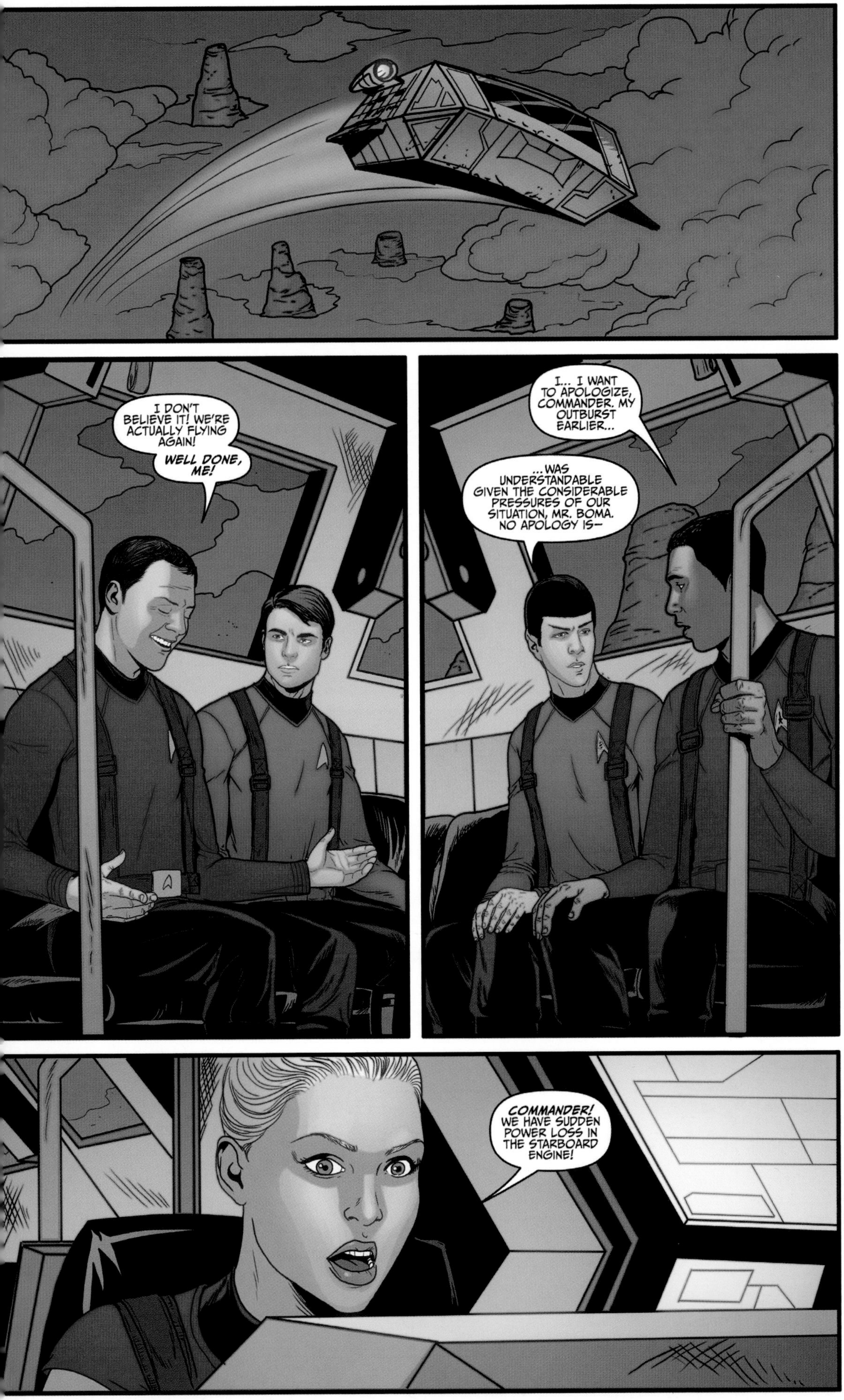

I DON'T BELIEVE IT! WE'RE ACTUALLY FLYING AGAIN!
WELL DONE, ME!
I... I WANT TO APOLOGIZE, COMMANDER. MY OUTBURST EARLIER...
...WAS UNDERSTANDABLE GIVEN THE CONSIDERABLE PRESSURES OF OUR SITUATION, MR. BOMA. NO APOLOGY IS—
COMMANDER! WE HAVE SUDDEN POWER LOSS IN THE STARBOARD ENGINE!

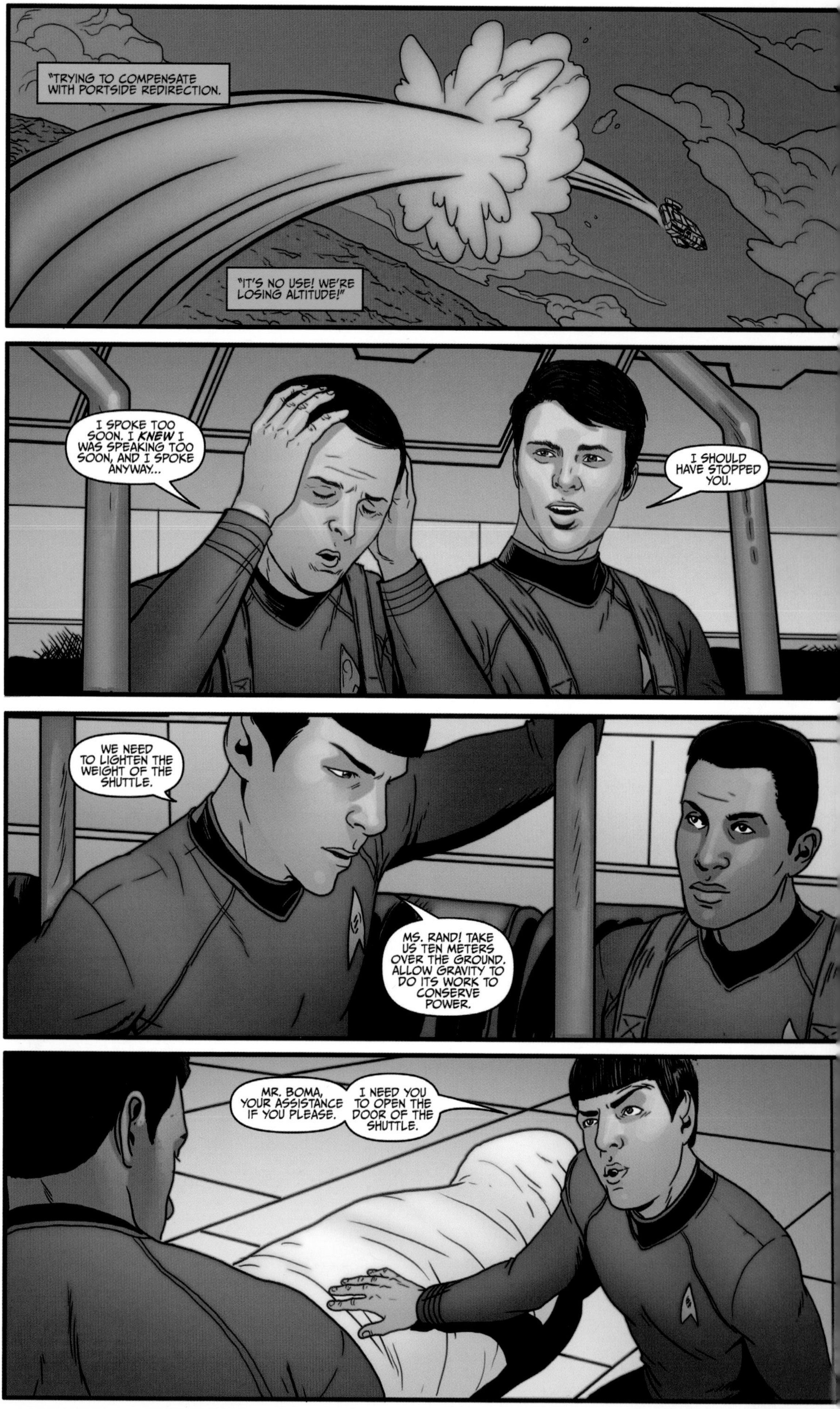

"TRYING TO COMPENSATE WITH PORTSIDE REDIRECTION.
"IT'S NO USE! WE'RE LOSING ALTITUDE!"
I SPOKE TOO SOON. I KNEW I WAS SPEAKING TOO SOON, AND I SPOKE ANYWAY...
I SHOULD HAVE STOPPED YOU.
WE NEED TO LIGHTEN THE WEIGHT OF THE SHUTTLE.
MS. RAND! TAKE US TEN METERS OVER THE GROUND. ALLOW GRAVITY TO DO ITS WORK TO CONSERVE POWER.
MR. BOMA, YOUR ASSISTANCE IF YOU PLEASE.
I NEED YOU TO OPEN THE DOOR OF THE SHUTTLE.

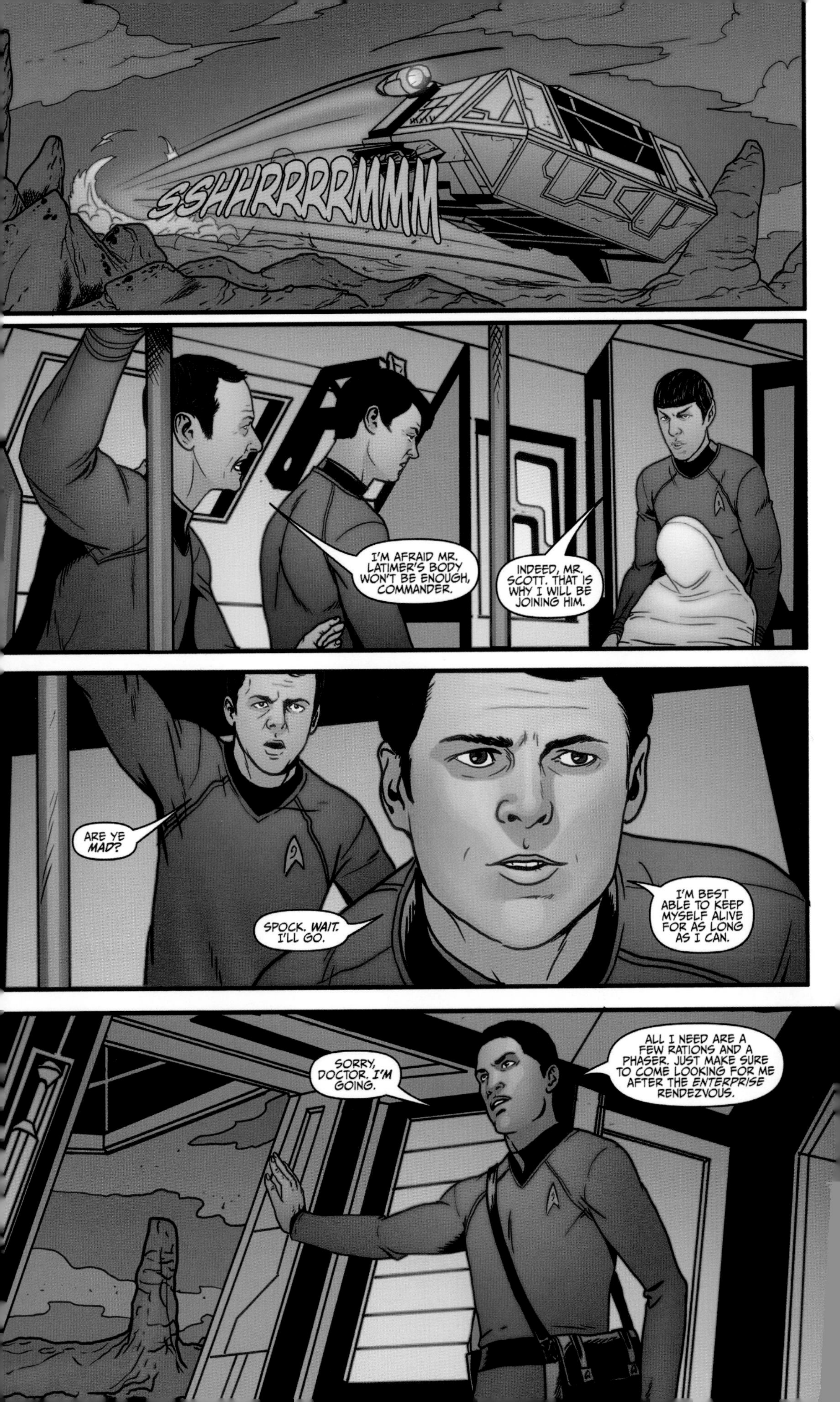
SSHHRRRRRMMM
I'M AFRAID MR. LATIMER'S BODY WON'T BE ENOUGH, COMMANDER.
INDEED, MR. SCOTT. THAT IS WHY I WILL BE JOINING HIM.
ARE YE MAD?
SPOCK. WAIT. I'LL GO.
I'M BEST ABLE TO KEEP MYSELF ALIVE FOR AS LONG AS I CAN.
SORRY, DOCTOR. I'M GOING.
ALL I NEED ARE A FEW RATIONS AND A PHASER. JUST MAKE SURE TO COME LOOKING FOR ME AFTER THE ENTERPRISE RENDEZVOUS.

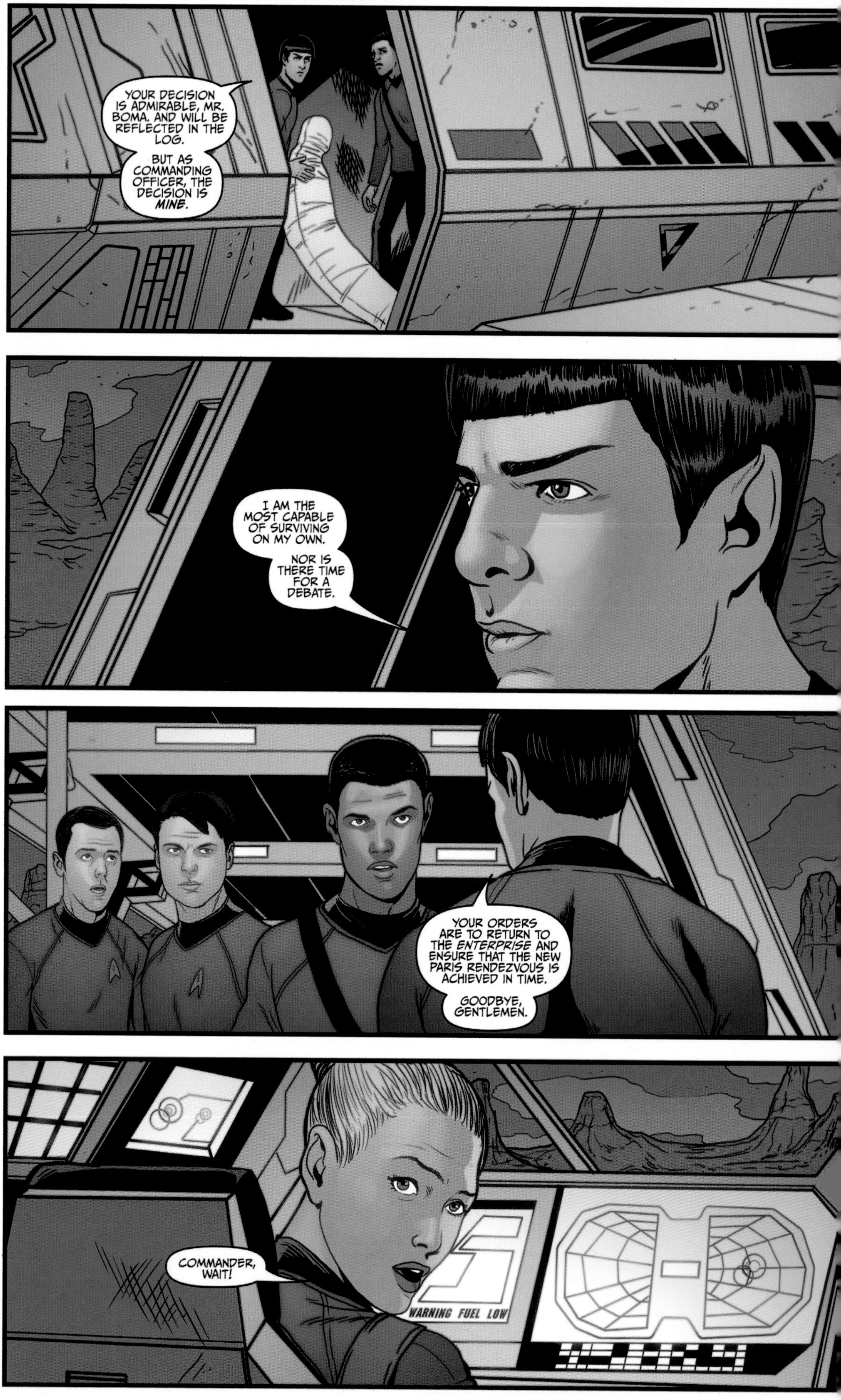
YOUR DECISION IS ADMIRABLE, MR. BOMA. AND WILL BE REFLECTED IN THE LOG.
BUT AS COMMANDING OFFICER, THE DECISION IS *MINE*.
I AM THE MOST CAPABLE OF SURVIVING ON MY OWN.
NOR IS THERE TIME FOR A DEBATE.
YOUR ORDERS ARE TO RETURN TO THE *ENTERPRISE* AND ENSURE THAT THE NEW PARIS RENDEZVOUS IS ACHIEVED IN TIME.
GOODBYE, GENTLEMEN.
COMMANDER, WAIT!
WARNING FUEL LOW

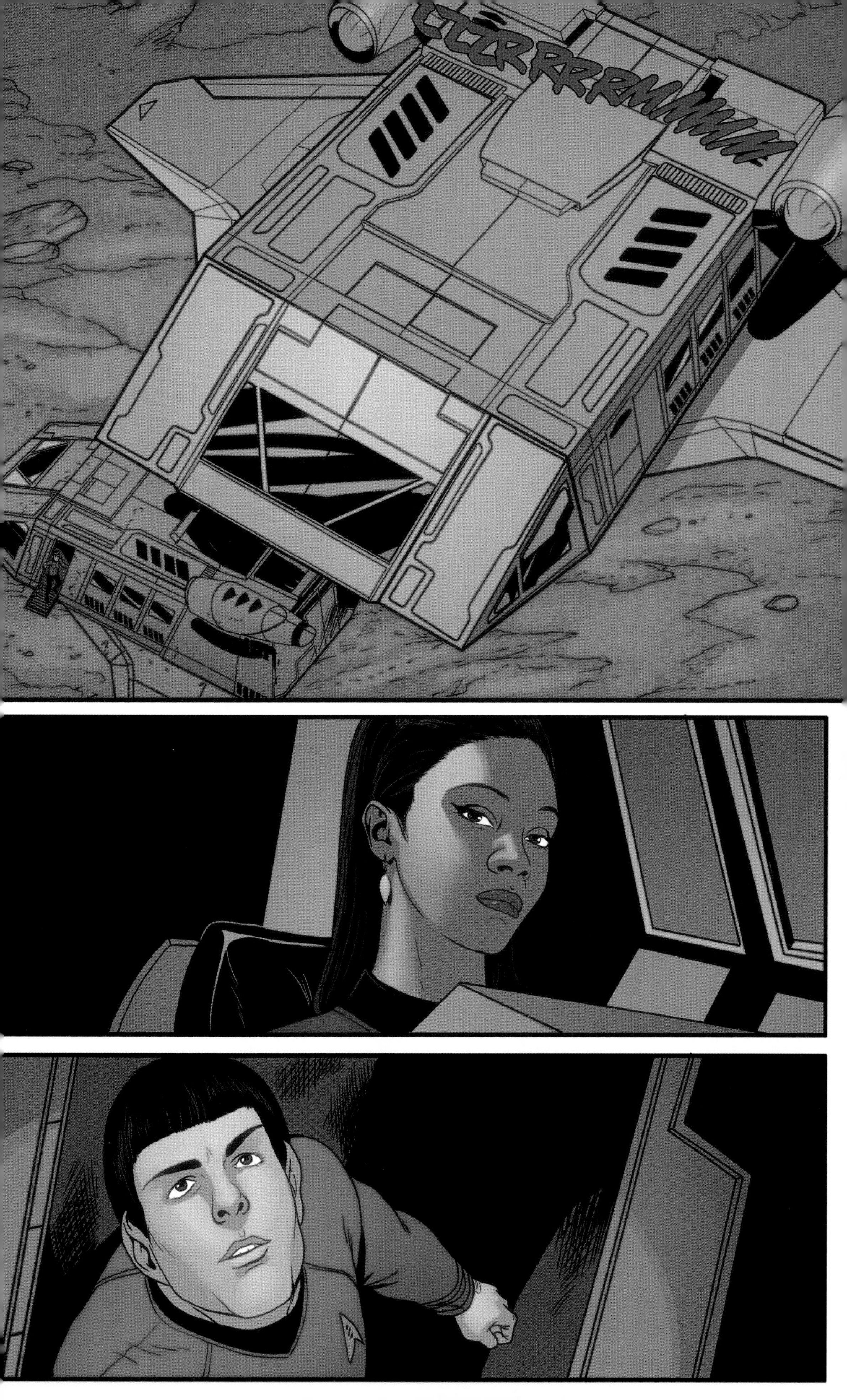

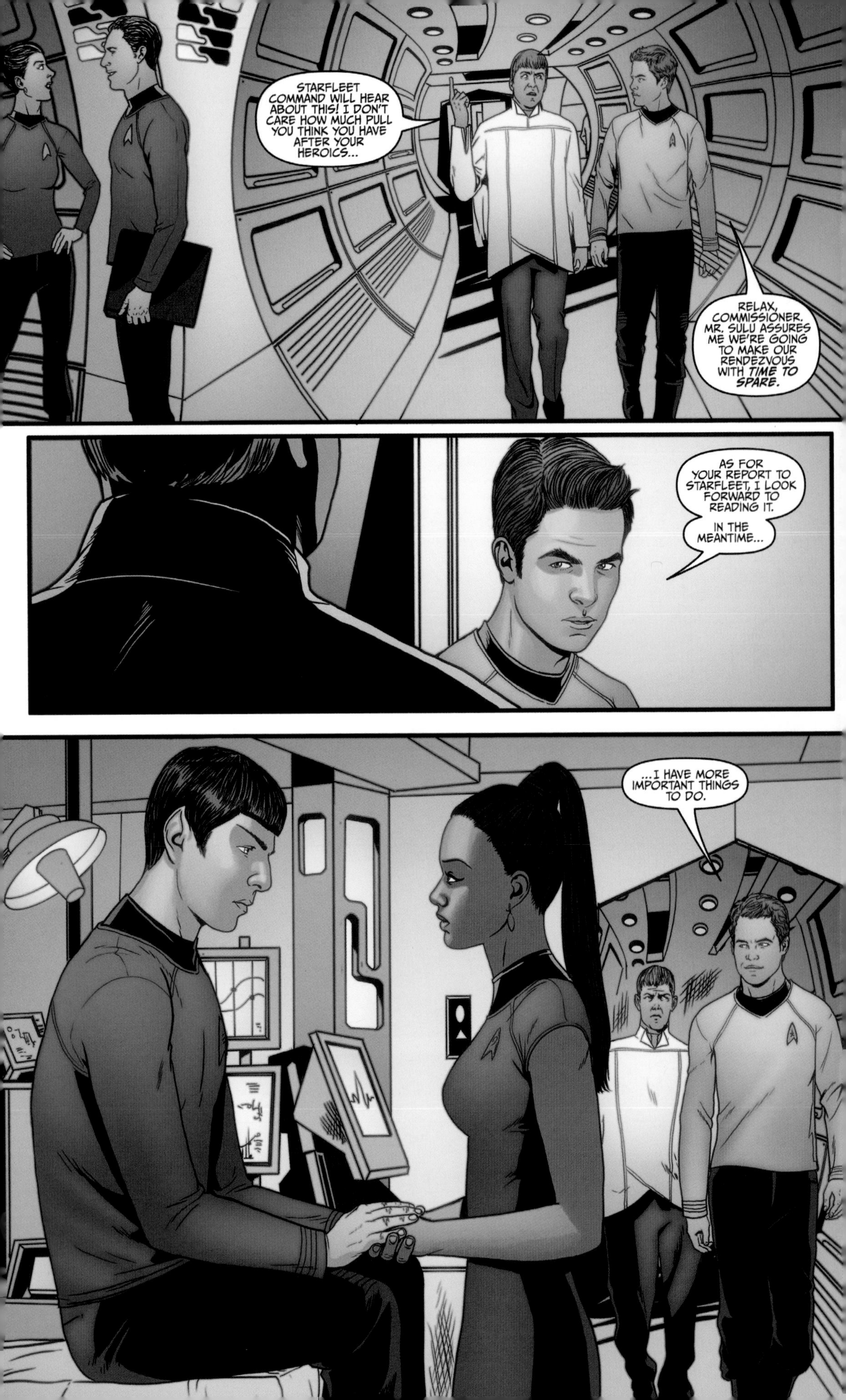
STARFLEET COMMAND WILL HEAR ABOUT THIS! I DON'T CARE HOW MUCH PULL YOU THINK YOU HAVE AFTER YOUR HEROICS...
RELAX, COMMISSIONER. MR. SULU ASSURES ME WE'RE GOING TO MAKE OUR RENDEZVOUS WITH *TIME TO SPARE.*
AS FOR YOUR REPORT TO STARFLEET, I LOOK FORWARD TO READING IT.
IN THE MEANTIME...
...I HAVE MORE IMPORTANT THINGS TO DO.

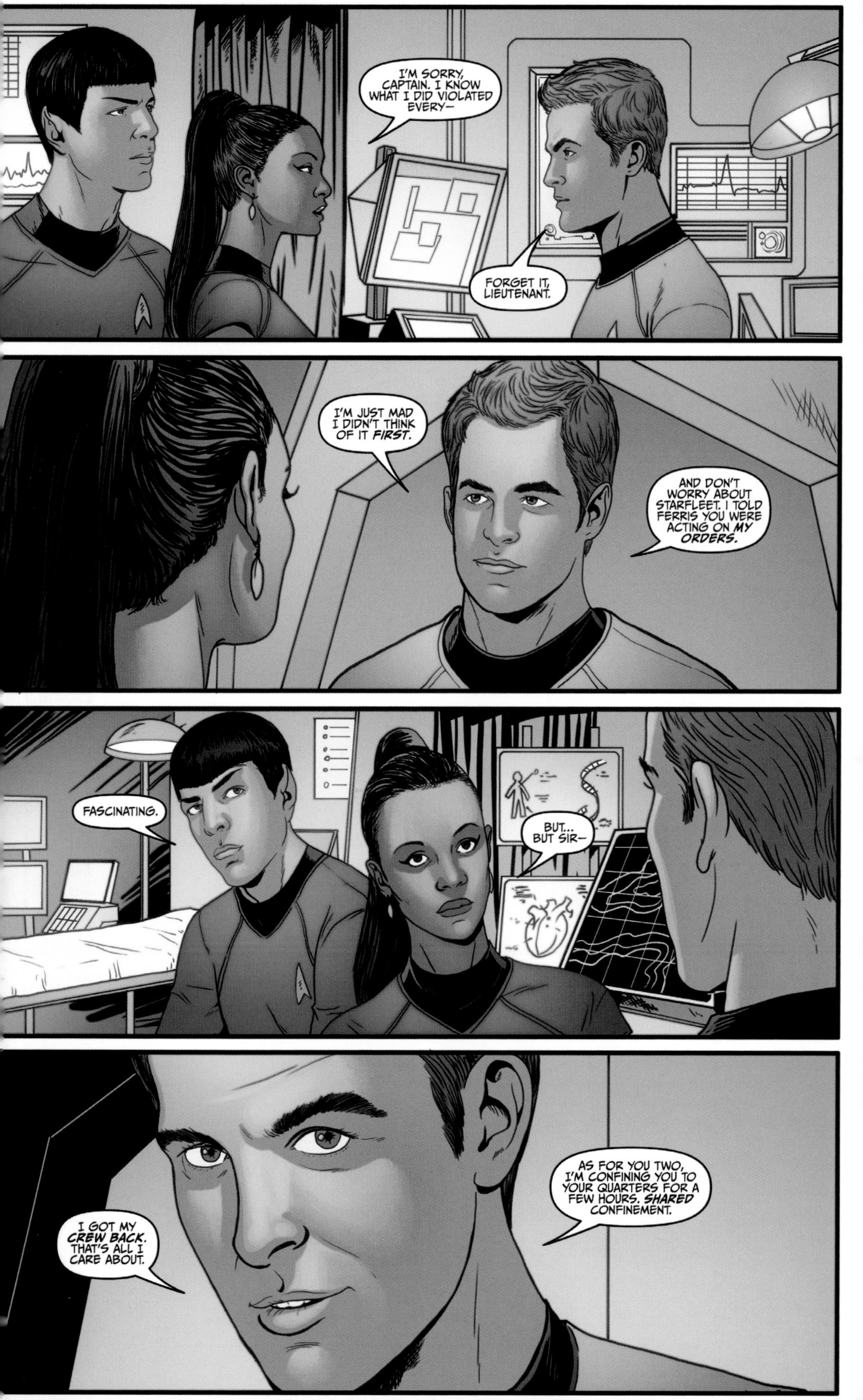
I'M SORRY, CAPTAIN. I KNOW WHAT I DID VIOLATED EVERY–
FORGET IT, LIEUTENANT.
I'M JUST MAD I DIDN'T THINK OF IT FIRST.
AND DON'T WORRY ABOUT STARFLEET. I TOLD FERRIS YOU WERE ACTING ON MY ORDERS.
FASCINATING.
BUT... BUT SIR–
I GOT MY CREW BACK. THAT'S ALL I CARE ABOUT.
AS FOR YOU TWO, I'M CONFINING YOU TO YOUR QUARTERS FOR A FEW HOURS. SHARED CONFINEMENT.

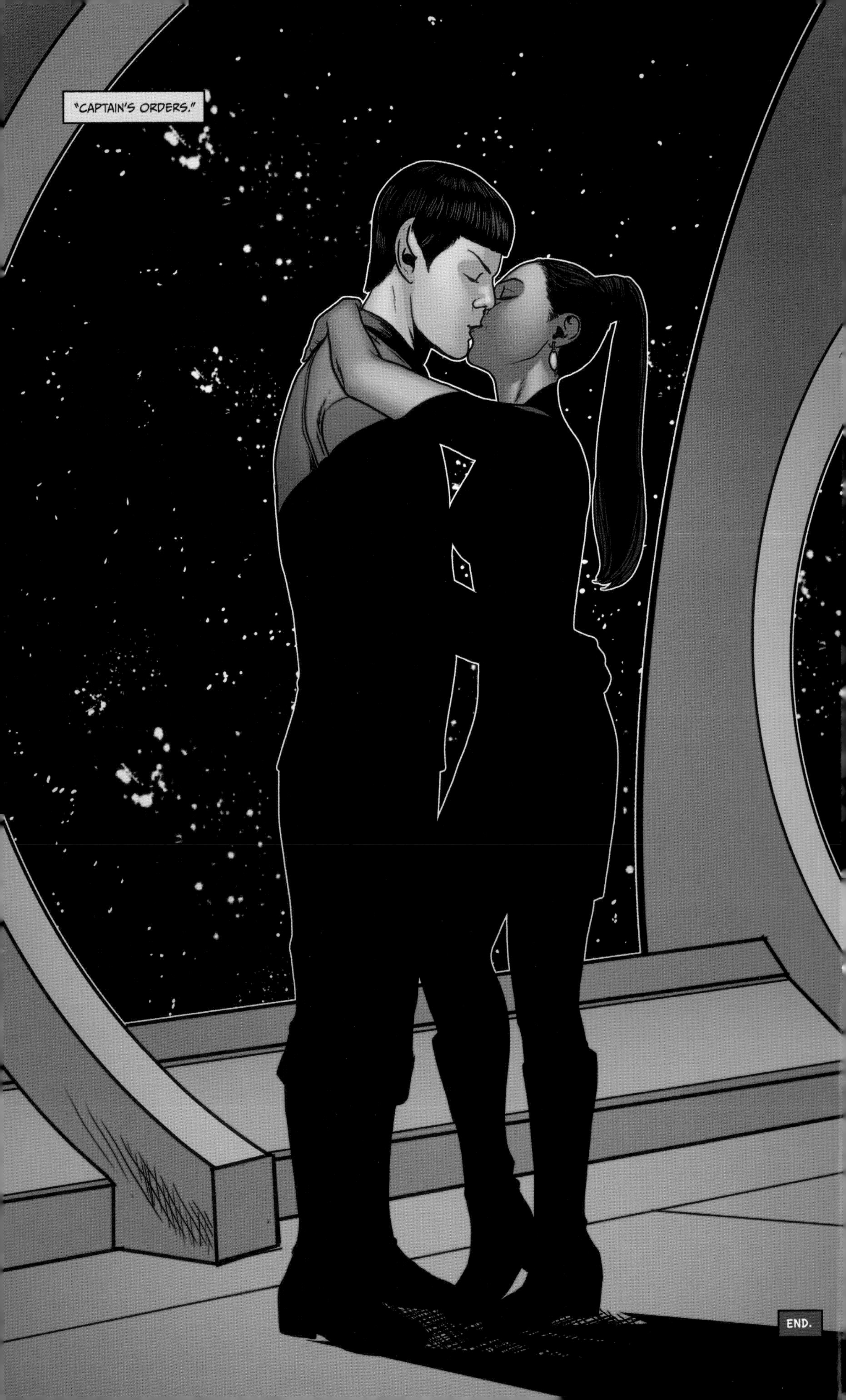
"CAPTAIN'S ORDERS."
END.